The legend of King Arthur has come down to us out of the dim mists of history. All we know for certain is that when the Romans left Britain a warrior chief led a band of brave followers against the Saxon invaders. Around his heroic deeds grew the legend of Arthur and Excalibur, of Merlin and the Knights of the Round Table.

Like all good legends it has grown with the telling and who is to say that so brave a company would not also have found time to undertake adventurous deeds on behalf of the weak, the poor and the oppressed?

These are some of the stories from the legend. They may not have happened at all—but we can hope they did.

A certain amount of artist's licence has been found necessary in preparing the illustrations, in view of the lack of precise information about the period.

Mysteries of **Merlin**

by DESMOND DUNKERLEY

with illustrations by
ROBERT AYTON

Ladybird Books Loughborough

THE SWORD IN THE STONE

In the hall of his palace old King Uther Pendragon of Britain lay dying. His queen Igraine knelt at his bedside while at the foot stood the wizard Merlin, white with age and in his eyes the calmness of great learning and wisdom. Around the dimly lit hall all the great nobles and knights of the land were gathered, talking together in urgent whispers for it was a time of great trouble in the kingdom.

For years past the Saxon pirates had been raiding the coasts, burning and killing. Even now the smoke from their latest attack could be seen in the sky to the west. Only the bravery and daring of King Uther had prevented them from marching far inland, for he had met and defeated them in countless battles, driving them back to the beaches and their long ships. The king's courage had set an example to other neighbouring kingdoms and together they had fought to hold back the Saxon tide.

But now the great king was dying, and had not yet named his successor. Each of those other kings was here now, hoping to be named by Uther as the next King of Britain.

5

The hall became suddenly silent as the dying king tried to speak. Queen Igraine clasped the frail hands, and Merlin moved to support the king's head as he attempted to raise himself up. All clustered forward around the bed to hear the king's words. All, that is, except a tall, beautiful woman with a haughty face and eyes as hard and as bright as diamonds: Morgan le Fay, the king's step-sister. She was so sure that her son Mordred, who stood beside her now, would be named as the next king that she was content to wait quietly in the background. Many said that she possessed magical powers almost as strong as those of the great Merlin himself, and so they feared her and kept away from her.

The king's weak voice could scarcely be heard in the large hall.

"With God's blessing I wish my son to take this kingdom after me, and all that have followed me should follow him also."

Even as the king fell back dead onto his pillows there was an excited outburst of talk. Men looked in amazement at each other for they knew of no son of Uther. Only the queen and Merlin were silent. The queen let her head fall gently onto the dead king's folded hands, while Merlin stood waiting for the uproar to cease. Before he could speak however the cold, hard voice of Morgan le Fay rang through the hall.

"This cannot be, for Uther had no son. My own son Mordred is by birth the rightful king."

The uproar started again for all thought this was true, though most did not want Mordred for their king. Merlin raised his hand.

"All will be made clear, lords, if you will but be patient. We will meet again in three weeks' time, on Christmas Day, in the great church of St Paul. Your rightful king will then be shown to you."

The crowd began to leave the great hall, some singly, some in groups. Many who had served and loved the dead king and fought beside him stood for a moment silently at his bedside as they passed. Others who had hoped to be the new King of Britain left without a glance, still muttering angrily amongst themselves.

Merlin watched until all were gone. Then he raised the kneeling queen to her feet and together they stood looking down at the bed. Suddenly Morgan le Fay spoke harshly from the shadows.

"I tell you again, old man, that this shall never be. There is no son but mine, and he alone shall rule Britain!"

Queen Igraine shivered but Merlin's eyes were steady as he watched Morgan le Fay leave, followed by her son.

As it neared the Feast of Christmas men began to make their way to the church of St Paul from all over the land. Nobles and common people alike were flocking to find out who was to be their next king.

On Christmas Eve the town was alive with the clank of arms and the tramp of men as powerful kings, princes and lords arrived with their followers. The narrow streets were crowded with citizens and soldiers, excitedly waiting for the next day.

Long before the dawn of Christmas Day all began to make their way toward the great church which stood just outside the town, amid wide fields.

Among those journeying in from outside was a knight named Sir Ector of Morven. His castle and lands were not far off and he had set out only that morning with his son, Sir Kay, and Sir Kay's foster-brother, Arthur. Sir Ector rode silently. He had been a close friend and companion of King Uther and carried the scars of many a fight with

the Saxons. Now, as he rode, he thought of those times, and of the dangers awaiting a country without a king. He wondered which of the great lords, who were already quarrelling amongst themselves, would conquer the others and take the crown of Britain for himself. He feared that it would be one not strong enough or brave enough to lead the constant fight against the Saxon menace. Above all he feared Morgan le Fay and the dark, silent Mordred, for it was rumoured that they had friends among the Saxon chiefs and might even ask for their help in winning the kingdom.

Sir Ector's thoughts brightened suddenly as he remembered Merlin. He had known the old man for as long as he could remember and trusted him in all things.

If Sir Ector was silent, Sir Kay and Arthur certainly were not. They were excited at the thought of the great day before them and talked eagerly, stopping only when one challenged the other to a race to a tree along the way.

"When this is over," said Sir Kay breathlessly after one such gallop, "I shall join Sir Bedivere's war-band against the Saxons. You may come with me if you wish, and carry my lance," he said, turning to Arthur.

Arthur was unusually silent for a second or two.

"I'll carry no man's lance," he said softly, "nor join another man's troop. The lance I carry will be my own, and I will lead my own war-band!"

Sir Kay roared with laughter, making his horse rear and shy.

"You, who have only twice fought the Saxons, lead a war-band against them? That's likely, I must say! Why, your sword's blade is barely dented. Now mine . . ." and Sir Kay dropped his hand to his side to draw the blade. Then he made a sound of annoyance.

"My sword! I've forgotten my sword! In all the rush to get away I forgot my sword!"

"A fine member of Sir Bedivere's warriors you would make," laughed Arthur. "But fear not, you shall have your sword. I will ride back now for it." He wheeled his horse and galloped back to the castle only to find it was locked and barred, for all had gone to the town.

"Kay shall have my sword," thought Arthur and set off back as fast as he could. When he reached the town he found the streets empty and deserted, for the people had assembled in the fields at the back of the church, and in the great

church itself. Arthur had passed through the churchyard when he stopped suddenly in amazement.

"Now here is a marvel," he thought. There at the very edge of the churchyard, beneath an ancient spreading yew tree, was a great granite stone. Set solidly in the stone was an anvil and from it jutted a magnificent sword.

"Kay shall have a sword after all!" thought Arthur. Reaching out, he pulled at the hilt and the sword slid easily from the anvil. He set off with his prize to search for Sir Kay, and found him anxiously waiting for Arthur.

"Where got you this?" he asked in astonishment as Arthur gave the great sword into his hand.

Before Arthur could answer, another voice echoed the question, and Merlin appeared beside them. He took the sword from Sir Kay, then looked at Arthur.

"Get you back inside and follow me not," he commanded. With that he disappeared amongst the high grass and shrubs of the churchyard taking the sword with him.

Hardly had the old man disappeared than the great doors of the church swung open before them and a great throng of knights and noblemen poured out.

"Where is Merlin?" they were asking. "It is time to explain. Where is Merlin?"

Sir Kay led them to the wizard who was now standing beneath the ancient yew tree beside the great stone. Arthur saw that the sword was again firmly embedded in the anvil. The crowd pushed and jostled and a huge circle formed around Merlin and the stone. When the hubbub of excitement ceased Merlin pointed to some words which were engraved around the base of the stone. He read them out clearly for all to hear.

"Whosoever pulls this sword from the stone shall be the rightful king of England."

whosoeuer pulls this sword from

The buzz of excited talk rose again as the lords and princes pushed their way forward to try. As each made his attempt the noise ceased, only to break forth again as the crowd saw he had failed. Merlin insisted that all the knights there should also make an effort to withdraw the sword, though Sir Ector did so unwillingly.

At last all had tried and the sword was still in the stone. Then Merlin spoke again.

"Now do you try!" he called loudly and clearly, pointing to Arthur who was standing at the edge of the crowd. There were murmurs and shouts of disapproval, for Arthur was not yet even a knight and was unknown to most. Some, like Sir Kay, laughed openly.

Merlin repeated his command and Arthur stepped forward. The silence as he lightly gripped the sword turned into a roar of amazement as the sword slid out easily.

It was several minutes before Merlin's voice could again be heard, calling for silence above the angry shouts of those who would not believe that the unknown youth who had beaten them could be their next king.

"How can this be, Merlin?" shouted King Lot of Orkney, angrily.

"Ay, what trickery is this?" called King Mark of Cornwall, and the shout was taken up by others.

"No trickery, lords," replied Merlin, "but before you learn all, let the same test be performed again at the next three feast days, so that none may doubt the issue."

It was agreed that they should meet again at Twelfth Day, Candlemas, and Easter. Four trustworthy knights were chosen to guard the stone by twos, and Sir Ector and Sir Bedivere began this duty.

At the next two feast days, Arthur was still the only one who could draw the sword from the stone. So when Easter came, the day set for the final test, the crowd was enormous. Only King Mark, King Lot and Mordred were going to try once more. All others had by now accepted that the honour was not for them.

Each of the three contenders came forward in turn, and heaved and pulled with all his might, while the watching thousands held their breath. Then each in turn had at last to stand down: Mordred sullenly, King Lot angrily, and King Mark silently as if admitting defeat.

Then, amid a stillness so complete that a lark's song could be heard from high above, Arthur stepped forward. Again the sword slid out easily into his hand with but the slightest whisper of metal.

As he held the sword high above his head the stillness was shattered by a mighty roar from the throats of the thousands of common people.

whosoever pulls this sw

"Arthur shall be our king! Arthur! Long live King Arthur!"

Realising that they could delay no longer, most of the nobles knelt before the new king and swore to serve him faithfully. Some, still angry and disappointed, strode away muttering darkly to themselves, but of Morgan le Fay and Mordred there was no sign.

The new king was escorted into the great church there to be crowned with great ceremony. When this was done, Merlin explained the mystery of the unknown youth who was now king of England. He told how, long ago, he had discovered a plot to kill the first-born son of King Uther and Queen Igraine. Merlin had taken the baby to the king's lifelong friend, Sir Ector, who had brought him up as his own, knowing nothing of his royal birth.

Then King Arthur, attended by all his nobles and knights, rode into the town amid great rejoicing, and set about preparing to make his kingdom safe.

THE ROUND TABLE

The new king had much to do. In the months since Uther's death, while Britain had no king, the Saxon pirates had become bolder and their raids more frequent. Their long ships were not only landing on beaches all round the coast, they were now sailing far up the rivers and landing their fierce warriors deep in the rich countryside. The Saxons were even starting to settle down, building their own villages and fortifying them.

To make matters worse some of the powerful lords who hated the young king, and who had left before his coronation, had banded together to try to seize the throne by force.

So King Arthur had decided to move his court further to the west, to the fortress town of Camelot which the Romans had built. From here it was but two days' march on the straight Roman roads to the new Saxon settlements in one direction, and to the lands and castles of the rebel lords in the other direction.

Hardly had the move been made than the king received disturbing news from both places. Just as an exhausted rider on a mud-spattered horse was gasping out news of two new Saxon landings, a commotion was heard in the courtyard below.

A second rider was brought before King Arthur with a message from the neighbouring kingdom of Cameliard. King Leodegrance of Cameliard had been a friend and ally of King Uther, and one of the first to acknowledge Arthur as the new and rightful King of Britain.

He now sent for help. Before the rebel lords could attack Arthur they would have to pass through Cameliard, and their armies were even now gathering on its borders. They far out-numbered the armies of King Leodegrance who

was, nevertheless, making ready to hold them off.

King Arthur immediately called a war council to make plans to meet the double threat. One army led by Sir Bedivere was to ride south to attack the Saxons, while King Arthur himself would lead a second to the aid of King Leodegrance. Sir Kay, with Merlin to support him, was to stay behind and command the garrison at Camelot.

All was hustle and bustle throughout the night, and the streets of Camelot echoed to warlike sounds as the armies made ready to leave.

Sir Bedivere left before dawn, for he had furthest to march. Later that morning King Arthur himself, mounted on his white charger, rode out of Camelot at the head of his knights. They made a proud sight, with pennants fluttering at every lance-head. As the trumpets sounded, the people of Camelot crowded the streets and windows to cheer and wave, for once more they had a king of whom they could be proud.

The army marched throughout the day and did not camp that night but pushed on hard towards Cameliard. Early the next morning, a rider from King Leodegrance met them with the news that the rebel army was drawn up for battle not an

hour's ride away. It was as well they had not camped, for even now they would barely be in time. They spurred on until, from the other side of a hill in front of them, they heard the clash of steel, the whinnying of frightened horses and the shouts of fighting men. They topped the rise and saw, spread out before them, the battle already joined. The white helmets of the soldiers of King Leodegrance were clearly to be seen and his army seemed hard pressed.

Setting himself at the head of his knights, who were spread out in a long line along the crest of the hill, Arthur ordered his trumpeter to sound the charge. As the first notes of the trumpet cut through the air, Arthur and his army swept downhill in a thunderous charge and crashed into the ranks of the rebels. Right through they rode, turned, and rode back again.

Sword took the place of lance and the fighting became fierce and hand to hand, with King Arthur himself always in the thickest of it. Many good knights fell that day, among them old Sir Turquine, boyhood friend of King Uther. He died beside Arthur, fighting for the son as he had fought for the father.

All day long the battle raged until, as the sun set, it seemed as if neither would gain the upper hand. Then suddenly King Arthur found himself face to face with a giant of a man in black armour, mounted on a black horse, and a crimson raven emblazoned on his shield. It was none other than King Pellinore himself, leader of the rebels and a sworn enemy of Arthur ever since the day he first drew the sword from the stone.

He recognised Arthur at once and came at him furiously with a great roar of rage, wielding his mighty two-handed sword. The mass of fighting soldiers parted around them, content to let the issue rest on the contest between these two. It was a contest that looked unequal, for the young king was dwarfed by his huge opponent. But Arthur was light and quick, while Pellinore was tiring fast. Suddenly it was all over. Seeing an opening, Arthur dashed inside the other's mighty swings, and ran the rebel king through.

As their leader fell dead, King Pellinore's men laid down their weapons. Those of their leaders still alive were brought before Arthur and surrendered their swords to him. He showed mercy to them by sparing their lives and they, in turn, swore to serve him in the future.

That night there was a great feast at the court of King Leodegrance to celebrate the victory. The rejoicing was complete when news came that Sir Bedivere had completely defeated the Saxons, burnt their towns and driven the survivors into the sea.

During this great banquet King Leodegrance was attended by his daughter, the Princess Guinevere, whom King Arthur thought the most beautiful lady he had ever seen. And Guinevere, for her part, cast many an admiring glance at the handsome young king whose brave deeds had saved her father's kingdom as well as his own.

As he left for Camelot the next morning at the head of his army, Arthur saw a hand wave from a window high in the castle and caught a glimpse of the same beautiful face. His thoughts were all of

Guinevere as he rode, for he had completely lost his heart. On his return he immediately sent Merlin to Cameliard to ask King Leodegrance for his permission to marry his daughter. Merlin, for some reason which he would not explain, warned King Arthur against the marriage, but for once Arthur would not listen to his old adviser.

King Leodegrance, however, was very happy to agree, and soon, to the great excitement of the people of Camelot, the Princess Guinevere arrived with her attendants. All was prepared for the wedding, and two days later King Arthur and the Princess were married with great ceremony.

As well as gifts of gold and a suit of silver armour, King Leodegrance sent an enormous table, made of oak and quite round, with places at it to seat two hundred and fifty knights. He also sent fifty of his own knights who were pledged to serve King Arthur.

As the king stood looking at the great round table he saw suddenly what a wise gift it was and how well he could use it. Since it was round none could sit at a higher place at the table than any other, and so none could think himself more in the king's favour than any other. Calling his knights to him, Arthur showed them the table.

"Let all who serve me, now take an oath of fellowship – the Fellowship of the Round Table!" he cried. The knights roared their approval.

"He who would take this oath step forward, and

solemnly swear to dedicate his life to chivalry, to the service of God and the protection of the weak and helpless!"

There was another roar of approval as every knight stepped forward. As Sir Ector, the first, raised his sword to take the oath, there was a sudden clap of thunder outside and the hall was plunged into deep darkness. Then light returned, and they were astonished to find that a name written in gold had mysteriously appeared at every seat around the table except one. Above that unnamed seat was written, "No one shall sit here save he be the world's truest knight."

All, even the king, looked to Merlin in their excitement, for he alone seemed calm.

"My lord king, and noble knights," he said solemnly, pointing to the strangely named place, "yonder is the Seat named Perilous." There was a moment's silence before the old man continued. "He that shall fill that seat is not yet here, nor yet

do even I, Merlin, know his name." With that the wizard took a cloth of gold silk from within the folds of his robe and placed it gently over the Seat Perilous.

Then the knights stepped solemnly forward, one by one, raised their swords hilt first in the sign of the Cross, and took their oaths. Then each took his named place: Sir Ector, Sir Kay, the brave Sir Bedivere, Sir Owen, Sir Gawaine and Sir Geraint, sons of a king of Wales, Sir Bors and Sir Balin, the twin sons of King Mark of Cornwall, and many others. Yet were there still many empty places.

When all were seated, King Arthur rose, younger than any there, and noble in his bearing.

"My lords," he proclaimed in a clear voice, "we will meet here on those same three feast days on which the sword was mine from the stone. Then shall we hear reports of high adventures undertaken and perhaps hear tell of new ones that await us. Then, too, may these empty seats be filled by those knights as yet unknown to us, who prove themselves worthy of our company."

Thus did King Arthur form his fellowship of the Knights of the Round Table whose fame was to spread throughout his kingdom and beyond.

EXCALIBUR

"It was a good idea of the king to hold a Tournament to celebrate his wedding," said Sir Kay, "even if it does mean a lot of work for me as Marshal."

Sir Owen nodded. "Aye, but there is more to celebrate than a wedding. The Saxons are gone – at least for a while – and the rebel Pellinore is dead."

"Both truly worth celebrating," agreed Sir Kay. The two knights were at the edge of the wide fields that stretched down from below the walls of Camelot to the river's edge. All around them workmen were busily erecting tents and marking out enclosures. Sir Kay looked at the bustle all around them. "Come," he said to his companion, "there is still much to do!" and they trotted their horses down to the lists, the long central arena where the main event of the Tournament would take place.

"Will you joust tomorrow to become the new queen's Champion?"

"Indeed I will," replied Sir Owen, "though more for the honour of taking part than for any hope of winning, for there will be many there stronger than I."

"But lacking your skill and your experience," said Sir Kay, clapping the other on the shoulder. "Though there will not be a Tournament to-morrow if the Lord Marshal does not busy himself." Together they rode off to direct the setting up of the Royal Pavilion.

The next day dawned bright and clear. The Tournament Field, gay with flags, was soon crowded with people who had flocked into Camelot from far and near. The archery and wrestling contests finished early so that all would be able to watch the jousting.

A fanfare of trumpets proclaimed that the king himself would open the contest. Arthur, wearing his new silver armour, sat on his white charger at one end of the lists.

"See how like a king he looks and fights!" the spectators said one to another, and they cheered as the king unhorsed one challenger after another.

"The king himself will be the queen's Champion," said Sir Kay to Sir Bedivere, ruefully rubbing his injured shoulder.

"It seems more than likely," agreed Sir Bedivere, watching the king riding up and down the lists challenging all comers.

Just as it seemed that there were no knights left to accept his challenge, a growing murmur of surprise spread from the far end of the lists.

"Who comes here?" asked Sir Bedivere.

"None that I know," replied Sir Kay. "His armour is plain, and neither his shield nor his helmet bears a crest."

"No pennant on his lance either," said Sir Owen. "Who can he be?"

The crowd watched in silence as the Unknown Knight raised his lance in salute and challenge before spurring his horse towards the king. They met with a crash that shattered both lances, though neither man was unhorsed. Riding back, they each collected a fresh lance. Again they met

and again, each time with a force that would have unseated a lesser man.

"Here is a worthy champion!" muttered Sir Kay.

"Worthy indeed," replied Sir Owen wonderingly, "but who is he?"

"We shall know soon enough," exclaimed Sir Bedivere excitedly. "See, they now fight on foot and at sword play the king has no equal, as the traitor Pellinore found to his cost."

But here was no Pellinore, but a swordsman as strong and as quick as Arthur himself. The fight raged up and down the arena with mighty blows dealt on either side. Suddenly, in front of the Royal Pavilion where Queen Guinevere sat, King Arthur raised his sword above his head.

"Enough! Enough!" he cried breathlessly. "We two are equal matched!" A great cheer rang round the ground as the Unknown Knight raised his sword also. When there was silence again the king spoke once more.

"It is not right that I, the king, should also be Champion at Arms to my lady the queen. That honour is yours, Sir Knight, and fairly won. But first, I pray you, make yourself known to us."

The Unknown Knight took off his helmet to reveal the handsome face of a young man no older than the king himself.

"Sire," he said, kneeling before King Arthur, "I am Lancelot of the Lake, from your realm in Brittany across the sea."

"Why came you here?" inquired the king.

"I had heard of your Majesty's Fellowship of Knights," replied Lancelot, "and came here to earn first a knighthood at your hands and then a place at your Round Table."

"Both have you earned and well," said the king, touching the kneeling figure on the shoulder with his sword. "Arise, Sir Lancelot of the Lake, and meet now the queen, whose Champion at Arms you are, by right."

Sir Lancelot thought that he had never in his life seen anyone more beautiful than Queen Guinevere as she smiled and placed the Champion's Sash around his shoulders. He knew in his heart he could never love another and swore to himself to serve her for as long as he lived.

Only two people were aware of the long glance which passed between the fair queen and her handsome young champion. Merlin saw and was troubled, yet he knew not why. Deeper in the crowd Morgan le Fay too saw Lancelot's love for the queen written on his face.

"There," she said in a triumphant whisper to her son Mordred, "there lies our way to bring about the downfall of Arthur!"

Later that evening Merlin looked for King Arthur. "He is resting in his tent, for he is weary after the jousting," Sir Bedivere told him. Merlin crossed the Tournament Field, which was still alive with people feasting and making merry in the glare of pine torches.

"Ah, my old friend," said the king, looking up with a smile as Merlin entered. "You find me mourning another friend, though not so old. See!" and Arthur held out his sword to Merlin. "See how my friend from the stone in the churchyard is now so bent and dented as to be useless. It is sad, is it not, that the sword that made me king should no longer be fit for a king to carry?"

"The sword did not make you king, sire," replied Merlin, "but only showed others your right to be so. Now that sword has served its purpose, but if you come with me now I will take you to a sword which will indeed be worthy of you."

45

Wearing a long robe over his armour Arthur followed Merlin, unnoticed by the crowds outside.

The lights and sounds of Camelot faded away in the distance behind them. The paths they took led through woods and wild places that Arthur had never seen before. Suddenly they were standing at the edge of a wide lake. A thin mist hung above the still surface of the water. No birds sang in the reeds and rushes around the lakeside, and only a rowing boat drawn up on the edge showed that any other person had ever been there before. Arthur shivered and pulled his cloak closer around his shoulders.

"What is this place?" he asked, half fearfully, for the stillness seemed magical and unnatural.

Merlin said nothing, but stood gazing out across the water. Arthur was about to repeat his question when the old wizard suddenly pointed with arm outstretched. "See there!" he said.

As Arthur's gaze followed the pointing finger he stepped back in amazement. Far out in the middle of the lake, in a patch of moonlight, a white clad arm rose up out of the water holding a sword!

"There is your sword!" said Merlin. "Take it now, for it is yours as long as you live."

The young king stepped into the boat and rowed quickly into the middle of the lake. Leaning out he gently took the sword and scabbard. At once the arm slid quietly out of sight beneath the water.

Arthur showed the sword to Merlin. He wanted to know how it came to be in the lake but the old man would tell him little. "It is called Excalibur – see that you are worthy of it. Guard well the scabbard also, for it has the power to protect from mortal wounds."

Turning the sword over and over in his hands Arthur found writing on either side of the blade. One said "Keep me!" and the other "Cast me away!"

"What does this mean?" asked the king in wonder. "Keep it I shall, but why should I ever cast away so marvellous a sword as this?"

"Only in the hour of your death do you return to this place and give back the sword," explained Merlin.

The way back seemed shorter but even so the first light of dawn was breaking over the towers and turrets of Camelot as Arthur and Merlin again reached the Tournament Field. Suddenly trumpets sounded from the battlements and a troop of armed men, led by Sir Kay and Sir Bedivere, clattered across the drawbridge towards them.

"We feared for your safety when we found your tent empty, yet your battered sword still there," explained Sir Kay later, as King Arthur sat with his knights at the Round Table.

The king stood and drew Excalibur from its scabbard. Holding it aloft he cried, "I have another sword now! May it never rest while any need its help and protection."

All his knights then rose also and King Arthur said, "Go now your separate ways. Carry word of our Fellowship and the oath we have made throughout my kingdom. Bring word back in one year's time from today when we will all meet again here.''

King Arthur, with Merlin by his side, watched them depart, and wondered what adventures each would have before they met again.